WALT DISNEY'S

The Prince
and the
Pauper

 BOOK ELEVEN

DISNEY PRESS

New York

Text adapted from *The Prince and the Pauper,*
written by Elizabeth Rudnick

Printed in China

First Edition
1 3 5 7 9 10 8 6 4 2

ISBN 978-1-4231-4903-3
T425-2382-5-11132

For more Disney Press fun,
visit www.disneybooks.com

ONCE UPON A TIME, there was a kindly king who ruled with fairness and generosity. His son, the prince, was busy with his studies, but he loved the kingdom, too. It was a time of great peace, and the people of the land were very happy.

But then the king grew sick and could no longer watch over his people.

Tyle

The greedy leader of the king's guards, Captain Pete, saw the king's illness as his chance to get rich. Day after day, the captain and his soldiers took food and money from the people of the kingdom.

One very cold morning, a peasant named Mickey watched as the royal coach drove past him. Mickey's dog, Pluto, spotted some sausages hanging from the back and ran after them. The coach disappeared through the palace gates, with Pluto following close behind.

"Stop!" Mickey shouted as he ran after his dog. "Come back!" But it was too late. The gates had shut behind Pluto.

When Mickey got to the gate, he asked if he could go inside to get his dog. The guard was about to say no when he got a good look at the peasant's face. "Your Majesty," the guard said, gasping. He quickly waved Mickey inside.

Mickey didn't notice what the guard had called him. He just wanted his dog back.

Meanwhile, inside the palace, the prince was sitting through a boring history lesson with Professor Horace. To amuse himself, he took out a peashooter and aimed it at his valet, Donald.

Whack! The prince landed a shot right on Donald's head. *Whack!* Another one hit the valet's bottom.

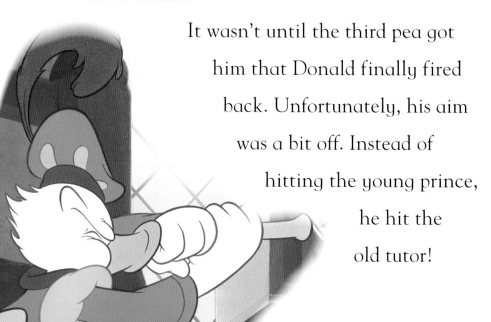

It wasn't until the third pea got him that Donald finally fired back. Unfortunately, his aim was a bit off. Instead of hitting the young prince, he hit the old tutor!

Professor Horace was about to scold Donald
and the prince when he heard a noise outside.
The prince ran to the window and looked down.
Captain Pete was holding a bag with someone
trapped inside. It was Mickey! The captain had
found him wandering around and captured him.
The prince ordered Pete to let the captive out of
the bag and send him inside.

Pete did as he was told, but the young pauper was so busy looking at everything around him that he soon got lost. Shiny suits of armor lined the walls. Crystal chandeliers hung from the ceiling. The whole palace gleamed. Mickey grinned with delight at the sight of his own reflection in the polished floor. He took a quick look around to make sure no one was watching, then kicked up his heels and danced a little jig.

Clang! Mickey bumped into a suit of armor. The helmet fell off and landed on his head. As he staggered around in the sudden darkness, Mickey bumped into another suit of armor, which toppled over onto another one, which toppled over onto another one . . .

Just then the prince entered the hall, and another helmet fell down—onto *his* head! Neither the prince nor the pauper could see where they were going. They walked blindly until—*bang!*—they crashed into each other. Slowly, they lifted the fronts of their helmets.

"You look just like me!" they shouted in unison.

The prince couldn't believe his luck. This was just the chance he had been waiting for! Now he could leave the boring palace and no one would know. He quickly convinced Mickey to trade places with him. To Mickey, the idea of living  in a luxurious palace as a prince sounded amazing. What harm could it do? They swapped clothes, and the prince headed for the door. "I'll be back in the blink of an eye," he promised.

The prince made it outside and hurried away to enjoy his day as a pauper. He tried playing fetch with some dogs, but they chased him over a fence. He tried to join a snowball fight, but it was three against one. Finally, he went to the market. There he saw one of the captain's guards stealing food from poor people.

"Halt! I am the prince," he cried and held up his royal ring. Then he climbed atop the cart and gave the food to the hungry peasants.

The guard took one look at the prince's ring and rushed back to tell Pete what had happened. When Captain Pete heard the news, he came up with a plan. He would get rid of the real prince and make the fake one do whatever he demanded.

Meanwhile, Mickey's friend Goofy had found the prince walking about town and brought him to his house. A while later, the church bells tolled throughout the land. The king had died.

The prince told Goofy that he was not Mickey, but the new ruler. He showed Goofy his ring. "I must go to the palace right away," he said. "It is my duty to take over as king." Then he leaped out of his chair and headed toward the door.

But Captain Pete was waiting for him just outside.

Pete's guards quickly captured the prince. They brought him to the palace, and threw him into the dungeon. Donald was already inside.

"I see your royal ring," Pete said from outside the prince's cell. "But it won't do you any good. As soon as the pauper is crowned king, I shall unmask him as an imposter and rule the kingdom myself!" And with an evil laugh, he left.

The situation looked hopeless for the prince— and for the entire kingdom.

Just then, a strange-looking guard came to the dungeon door. It was Goofy! He knocked out the guard and handed Donald the keys to the cell. "Sit tight, little buddy," Goofy told the prince.

While Donald struggled with the lock, Goofy kept an eye out for more guards. Finally, the cell door swung open. The prince, Goofy, and Donald took off, with Pete's guards close behind.

Meanwhile, Mickey was trying to avoid being crowned king. He knew that Captain Pete would keep stealing from the people of the kingdom, so he stopped the ceremony. "I'm the prince. So whatever I order must be done, right?" Mickey asked the man who was about to crown him. The man nodded, and Mickey ordered the guards to seize Pete.

But Pete was ready for this. "He is not the prince!" yelled the wicked captain. "He's an imposter. Seize *him*!"

"*I'm* not an imposter, though," came a voice from a high balcony. It was the real prince!

Everyone gasped and looked up as the prince

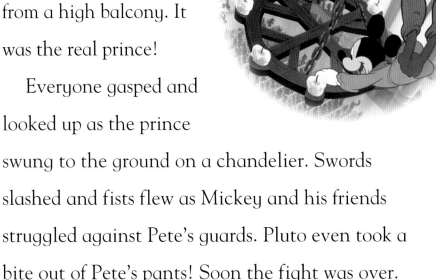

swung to the ground on a chandelier. Swords slashed and fists flew as Mickey and his friends struggled against Pete's guards. Pluto even took a bite out of Pete's pants! Soon the fight was over. The evil captain was arrested, and the prince was crowned king.

The kingdom was once again in kind, caring hands. With Mickey and Goofy by his side, the new king ruled . . . happily ever after.